Dear Parents:

Congratulations! Your child is taking the first steps on an exciting journey. The destination? Independent reading!

STEP INTO READING® will help your child get there. The program offers five steps to reading success. Each step includes fun stories and colorful art or photographs. In addition to original fiction and books with favorite characters, there are Step into Reading Non-Fiction Readers, Phonics Readers and Boxed Sets, Sticker Readers, and Comic Readers—a complete literacy program with something to interest every child.

Learning to Read, Step by Step!

Ready to Read   Preschool–Kindergarten
• big type and easy words • rhyme and rhythm • picture clues
For children who know the alphabet and are eager to begin reading.

Reading with Help   Preschool–Grade 1
• basic vocabulary • short sentences • simple stories
For children who recognize familiar words and sound out new words with help.

Reading on Your Own   Grades 1–3
• engaging characters • easy-to-follow plots • popular topics
For children who are ready to read on their own.

Reading Paragraphs   Grades 2–3
• challenging vocabulary • short paragraphs • exciting stories
For newly independent readers who read simple sentences with confidence.

Ready for Chapters   Grades 2–4
• chapters • longer paragraphs • full-color art
For children who want to take the plunge into chapter books but still like colorful pictures.

STEP INTO READING® is designed to give every child a successful reading experience. The grade levels are only guides; children will progress through the steps at their own speed, developing confidence in their reading.

Remember, a lifetime love of reading starts with a single step!

© 2016 Spin Master PAW Productions Inc. All rights reserved. Published in the United States by Random House Children's Books, a division of Penguin Random House LLC, 1745 Broadway, New York, NY 10019, and in Canada by Penguin Random House Limited, Toronto. PAW Patrol and all related titles, logos, and characters are trademarks of Spin Master Ltd. Nickelodeon and all related titles and logos are trademarks of Viacom International Inc.

Step into Reading, Random House, and the Random House colophon are registered trademarks of Penguin Random House LLC.

Visit us on the Web!
StepIntoReading.com
randomhousekids.com

Educators and librarians, for a variety of teaching tools, visit us at
RHTeachersLibrarians.com

ISBN 978-0-553-52288-4 (trade) — ISBN 978-0-553-52289-1 (lib. bdg.)

Printed in the United States of America

10 9 8 7 6 5 4 3 2 1

nickelodeon

PAW PATROL

Meet Tracker!

by Geof Smith

illustrated by Jason Fruchter

Random House 🏠 New York

4

Carlos is in the jungle.
He is digging
for lost treasure.

The PAW Patrol
will visit Carlos.

Carlos trips.

He drops his phone!

Carlos is in
a deep pit.
He yells for help.

A pup hears Carlos.

He runs to help.

His name is Tracker.

Tracker finds
Carlos's phone.

He calls the PAW Patrol.
They will help Carlos.

A snake!

Tracker is not afraid.
He chases the
snake away!

PAW Patrol to the rescue!

Chase pulls Carlos
out of the pit.
Carlos is safe!

Because he helped Carlos,
Tracker gets to join
the PAW Patrol!

Tracker gets a Pup Pack.

It has cool tools!

Ropes spring from Tracker's pack.

Tracker swings through the trees on his ropes!

Tracker gets
his own truck, too!

Welcome to the team, Tracker!